JÜRG OBRIST

MAX
AND
MOLLY

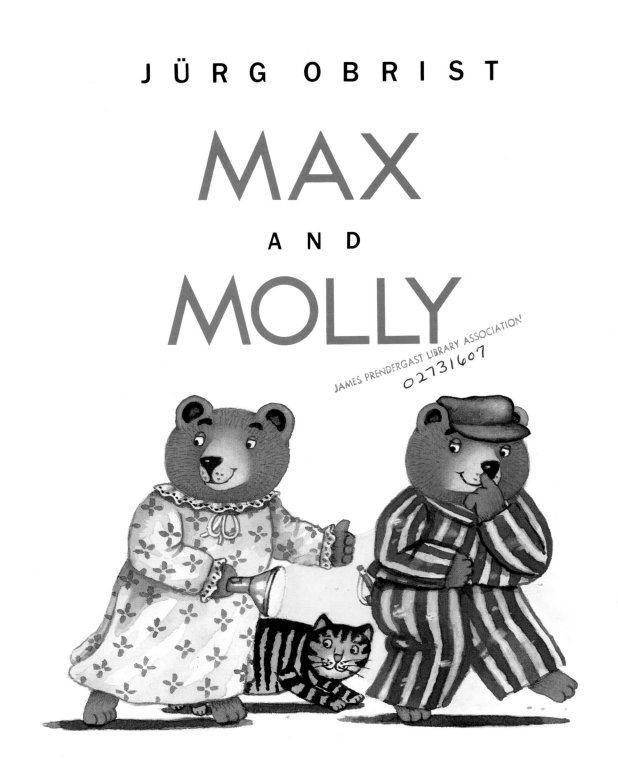

G. P. Putnam's Sons   New York

Many thanks to Lisa,
who was quite involved in this
funny honey business.
—J. O.

Copyright © 1989 by Jürg Obrist.
All rights reserved.
Published simultaneously in Canada.
Printed in Hong Kong by South China Printing Co.
Designed by Golda Laurens
Library of Congress Cataloging-in-Publication Data
Obrist, Jürg. Max and Molly.
Summary: Max and Molly try to find out who's
been stealing Grandpa's honey jars during the night.
1. Grandfathers—Fiction.   2. Honey—Fiction.
3. Bears—Fiction]   I. Title.
PZ7.014Max 1989 [E] 88–11397
ISBN 0–399–21630–8
First Impression

"Hi, Grandpa," Max and Molly called to
Grandfather Fur.
"Well, well! Look who's here," he said, and
smiled.

Every year Max and Molly spent August with their grandfather. And what a wonderful time they had together.

Grandpa never seemed to run out of exciting games to play, things to do, or friends to invite along for the fun. Everything was just the way the little bears liked it.

Except for one small thing: honey season! That's when Grandpa forgot all about fun and turned into a busy grouch.

"Uh, oh," said Max and Molly one morning when they woke up and saw Grandpa out in the backyard. "It's started! The honey must be ready to collect."

Soon Grandpa's kitchen looked like a wizard's laboratory. Grandpa stirred and mixed and cooked his honey for hours on end. There were jars everywhere. Jars with light honey and jars with dark honey. Jars with thin honey and jars with thick honey.

"It takes a lot of patience and skill to make a blend as tasty as mine!" Grandpa claimed.

Grandpa never stopped thinking about honey. Even in his sleep he had the sweetest honey dreams.

To make matters worse, Grandpa always had some tasks on hand for his little guests to do.

"Oh, phooey!" Max and Molly grumbled. "We're washing jars and chasing flies while everyone else is outside having a good time."

Honey, nothing but honey everywhere. Yet Max and Molly hardly got a taste of it.

"Unbearable," Max moaned.

"Patience," said Grandpa. "Honey needs to sit and ripen," he explained.

"It will get stale and moldy," Molly muttered.

"What a waste," Max sighed.

Finally the last jar was filled.

"Excellent in color, outstanding flavor," Grandpa announced proudly as he stored the jars in the kitchen cupboard.

"Hooray!" Max and Molly cheered. "Now that the honey is made, we can have some fun. Right, Grandpa?"

But BUZZING BEES! The next day a terrible
thing happened. One of Grandpa's honey jars was
missing!

"A robbery! A theft!" Grandpa roared.
"Someone is after my honey!"

Was it the mailman? Was it the lady next
door? Or was it . . . ?

Grandpa even eyed his little grandbears
suspiciously.

Who could it be? How did it happen? Grandpa
searched the kitchen until late that night, looking
for clues to the missing honey.

Before he went to bed, Grandpa locked the
cupboard and hid the key in the cookie jar. And
just to make sure, he pushed the bureau up
against the front door.

"That should do it," he said.

The next morning Grandpa almost fainted. The cupboard was wide open! Another jar had disappeared!

"Who is this crafty robber?" Grandpa shouted. "It's got to be someone who knew about the key in the cookie jar." And with that, he stared at Max and Molly.

"We have nothing to do with this sticky honey business," they assured him.

But Grandfather Fur had made up his mind. He hardly spoke to Max and Molly all day, and he sent them to bed early without their dinner.

"This is serious," Max sighed. "The only way out of this is to solve the mystery ourselves!"

So, as soon as they heard Grandpa's steady snoring through the bedroom wall, Max and Molly crept downstairs to the kitchen.

They sprinkled flour all over the floor.

"Now let's hide and see who comes," they whispered.

They waited and waited. . . .

Suddenly they heard footsteps. A shadow moved along the wall. Max and Molly held their breath.

By Sherlock! It was Grandpa walking in his sleep.

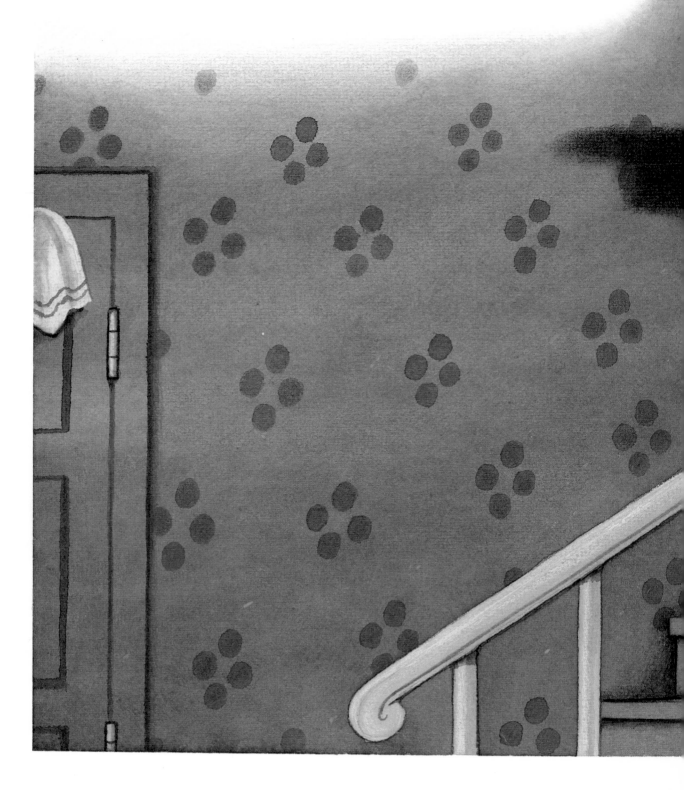

He was aiming for the cookie jar with the hidden
key. From there he went straight to the cupboard
where he helped himself to one of his precious
honey jars.

Back in his bedroom he gobbled up the
honey—just as he must have done for the past
two nights.

In the morning Grandpa discovered that a third jar was gone.

"That does it!" he snorted. His ears quivered. His snout grew bigger and bigger. "Max and Molly, you go pack your bags at once!"

But Max and Molly just smiled and pointed to Grandpa's big, clear footprints all over the kitchen floor.

In his bedroom they found the three empty jars under his bed.

"YOU are the honey thief, Grandpa," said Molly.

"YOU ate up your own honey in your sleep and thought it was all a delicious dream," said Max.

Grandpa scratched his ear. He twitched his nose.
Finally he stuttered, "My, oh my. I guess I really
did take this honey business too seriously. And I
even blamed you, my brave and clever bears, for
something I did myself. I'm sorry. But I'll make it
up to you, I promise."

Molly began to giggle. Grandpa started to chuckle. Then they all burst out laughing.

"Let's go out and have some fun," said Grandpa.

"Yippee!" cried Max and Molly.

That evening they sat together, laughing and
joking and eating all the honey they wanted. And
they sang:
    "Jars and jars of honey
    sticky, fresh, and yummy.
    It slides right down
    and moves around
    and makes us feel so funny!"